W9-BDK-485

# DINOSAUR ADVENTURE

by NORA LOGAN

illustrated by BERT DODSON

SCHOLASTIC INC.
New York Toronto London Auckland Sydney Tokyo

ISBN 0-590-33049-7

12 11 10 9 8 7 6 5 4 3 2        7 8/8

Printed in the U. S A.    11

*This book is for Roger.*

Scholastic Books in the Pick-A-Path Series

## How many have you read?

# READ THIS FIRST

Are you ready for some really fantastic adventures?

Start reading on **page 1** and keep going until you have to make a choice. Then decide what you want to do and turn to that page.

Keep going until you reach **THE END.** Then, you can go back and start again. Every path leads to a new story!

It is all up to you!

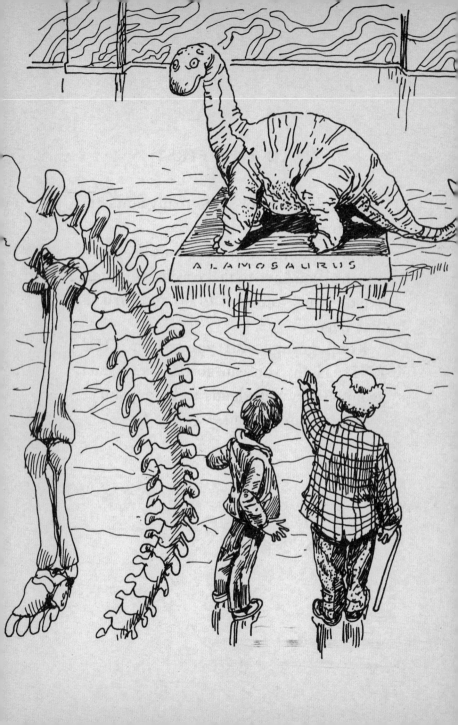

It's Sunday morning. You wake up early and eat your cereal very fast. You can't wait to meet your Uncle Max in town.

Max is a little nutty. He runs the prehistoric animal department at the museum. He also invents things. Last year he invented a laser can-opener, to open cans from across the room. And a bed that could make itself.

What will it be this time?

You find Max in his workshop at the museum, eating peanut butter and carrot sticks. "Have you met Alamo?" he asks, pointing to a fake dinosaur across the room. "The name is short for *Alamosaurus*."

*Turn to* **page 2.**

Alamo isn't much bigger than a pony. He has short legs and a long neck and tail.

"Today Alamo will help me to test my new invention," Max says. He digs into the pocket of his baggy pants and pulls out a small metal box. It looks like a tape recorder or radio.

"It's called a time beamer," Max announces proudly. He explains how it works, but you can't really understand all the long words.

"Never mind," says Max, "I'll show you."

Max reaches under his lumpy jacket and pulls out a red key on a shoelace. First he aims the machine at Alamo. Then he puts the key into a hole in the machine and twists.

*Go on to the next page.*

You see a greenish glow all around Alamo. A moment later, the baby dinosaur lifts its small, pointed head.

"You brought it to life!" you gasp.

"Not really," Max says. "The time beamer switched the fake dinosaur with a real one from 70 million years ago. It beamed the real animal forward in time."

Alamo walks up to you and sniffs at your sneakers. You get scared.

"Don't worry," says Max. "He only eats vegetables."

*Turn to* **page 4.**

Max offers Alamo some peanut butter. He gobbles it up, then sticks his head under Max's jacket, looking for more. "I'd better send him back now," says Max.

Max turns the key in the time beamer again. You notice that his hands are glowing. Your own body starts to throb. You look down and see that you have turned bright green! Then you black out.

*Turn to* **page 11.**

You roll down the cliff and land on a ledge about three feet wide.

Whew! You're safe for now. But you can't rest here forever. You feel weak from hunger. And you have to find Max.

You look up. You see a path that doesn't look too hard to climb. But when you reach the top, you'll have to face the flying creature again.

You look down. The path is much steeper and more dangerous.

*If you climb up, turn to* **page 27.**

*If you climb down, turn to* **page 18.**

Max sets the time beamer for 2984.
He twists the key and you both black out. When you wake up, you have trouble breathing. The ground is covered with concrete. You can't see any trees or flowers.

A hundred feet away you notice an orange spaceship, shaped like a saucer. Just outside there are two men, wearing plastic bubbles over their heads.

You and Max can hardly breathe now. Coughing and sputtering, you stumble toward the men, who help you into the spaceship. As the doors slide shut behind you, you see the time beamer on the ground outside. Max must have dropped it.

"The time beamer!" you scream. But it's too late. "Final call for departure to Zakbar," a deep voice booms. "Five . . . four . . . three . . . two . . . one . . . BLAST-OFF."

The spaceship rises silently into the sky.

Turn to **page 44.**

**8**     You jump on Alamo's back and hold tight, your arms around his neck. He gallops along the edge of the herd. But Alamo is much smaller than the others and he can't keep up. Soon you are at the back of the herd.

Now you can see what caused the stampede. A dozen very ugly dinosaurs are getting closer and closer. Their heads come to a point and they have red, beady eyes. They look mean.

*Go on to the next page.*

Alamo slows down as you get near the fern tree. You see that Max is safe, sitting on a branch of the tree. You urge Alamo forward. But he's too tired to go fast any more. Any second you'll be attacked.

You throw Max the key as you pass slowly under the tree. "Use the time beamer," you shout. "It's our only chance!"

You see Max catch the key. Then you close your eyes and pray.

*Turn to* **page 29.**

When you wake up, you and Max are beneath a tall fern tree. Across a field you see a herd of dinosaurs like Alamo only much, much bigger. They are grazing peacefully.

Even Max looks surprised. "Something must be wrong with the machine," he grumbles. He fiddles nervously with the key, which shines in the sunlight. Playfully, Alamo takes the shoelace in his mouth, then runs off with the key!

Your heart sinks. Without the key, you'll be stuck here forever!

"Let's run after him," you say to Max. But Max shakes his head. "Running gives me a headache. Besides, I'll figure something out."

You're afraid to leave Max. But you also don't want to lose the key.

*If you run after Alamo alone,*
*turn to* **page 16.**

*If you decide to stay with Max,*
*turn to* **page 13.**

**12**

You run toward the edge of the field. The earth shakes as the herd gets closer. You throw yourself down in the dirt just in time.

The herd of dinosaurs thunders by. When the dust clears, you head back to Max. You're worried that he might have gotten hurt.

You reach the fern tree. He's sitting under the tree, coated with dust. "Most interesting," he mumbles to himself as he writes in his notebook.

"I'm all right," you say to your uncle. But he doesn't seem to hear you. "I got the key back," you say a little louder. But he still doesn't look up.

"Max!" you shout at the top of your lungs. "I got the key back and I want to go home!"

*Turn to* **page 28.**

You decide to stay with Max. He isn't worried about getting back to the present. Why should you be?

"What an opportunity!" Max says. "For instance, look at these strange tracks. If we follow them we might find a totally new kind of dinosaur. Or a nest of eggs. We'll be famous!"

Max picks up a branch from the ground to use as a walking stick. Then he follows the tracks across the field. For half an hour, you follow Max. It's hard to keep up with him.

Suddenly a dark shadow crosses your path. Something is following *you*! You look up and see a flying creature like a giant lizard. It has a long, sharp beak and wings like a bat.

*Turn to* **page 15.**

Before you can scream, it swoops down and grabs you with its sharp claws. It all happens so fast that Max doesn't even know you are gone.

The creature carries you over a lake. You wriggle inside your jacket and get an idea. You could slip out of the jacket and dive into the lake. If you hit the water right, you might not get hurt. You could also stay with the creature and try to escape later. After all, you are not a very good diver.

*If you dive into the lake,
turn to* **page 21.**

*If you decide to stay with the flying
creature for now, turn to* **page 58.**

"Wait right here," you shout to Max. You run after Alamo as fast as you can. About halfway to the herd, Alamo stops to graze. When you catch up to him, he rubs his head against your chest. You notice the shoelace in the grass at his feet.

Hooray! The key is still on the shoelace. Now you can go back to Max. You pat Alamo good-bye. But then a sound like thunder makes you freeze.

*Go on to the next page.*

The herd of dinosaurs is running your way. Something must have frightened them. If you stay where you are, you'll get trampled. You could get on Alamo's back, and ride with the herd. Or you could try to run to the edge of the field before the herd reaches *you*. Either way, you have to act fast.

*If you get on Alamo's back,
    turn to* **page 8.**

*If you run toward the edge of the
    field, turn to* **page 12.**

**18**     Inch by inch you climb down the steep trail. Halfway down, you stop to rest. Over the treetops you see a lake. And beyond that you see a fern tree, taller than all the rest.

That's it! That is the very spot where you first arrived in the dinosaur age. You figure Max will go there when he sees that you are missing.

You get to the bottom of the cliff and start walking toward the fern tree. On the way, some glittery stones catch your eye. You bend down and put them in your pocket. An hour later, you reach the tree.

*Go on to the next page.*

Your guess was right. Max is stretched out in the shade. He sees you and waves. But he doesn't even ask where you've been.

"Time to move on," he says, getting to his feet. "I didn't find any eggs. But my bag is filled with bones. There's no doubt about it; I'll be famous when we get home."

"We'll never get home," you say. "Alamo took the key, remember?"

"You worry too much," Max replies. "I found a bunch of paper clips and wire in my pocket. It didn't take long to make a new key. See?"

*Turn to* **page 20.**

**20** Sure enough, Max holds up another key. Then he takes out the time beamer and fits the key inside.

You're more than ready to go home. But Max has another idea. He wants to make a quick trip to the future.

*If you go back to the present time, turn to* **page 54.**

*If you decide to visit a future time zone, turn to* **page 7.**

You make a perfect dive into the water, leaving your jacket in the flying creature's claws. Then you swim to the edge of the lake. Your Uncle Max is walking by, still following the tracks.

"Max!" you shout. "Am I glad to see you."

Max looks at your dripping clothes. "Did you have a nice swim?" he asks.

"Not exactly." You try to explain what happened. But Max interrupts.

"Tell me later," he says. "First you have to dry off." And he leads you to a sandy spot in front of a boulder. Half of the boulder is hidden in the trees.

*Turn to* **page 22.**

You lean against the greenish stone and dig your feet into the sand. You start to explain about the flying creature. But suddenly the rock moves behind your back.

Oh, no! It must be an earthquake!

But it isn't. And the rock isn't a rock. It's a dinosaur — and it is standing up.

You tumble to the ground and land between the animal's legs. Its foot is bigger than you are.

You look up and see Max hanging on to a tiny arm that grows out of the dinosaur's chest.

*Turn to* **page 24.**

"I'm safe here," Max yells. "He can't move this arm very high and he can't reach me. But you stay out of sight. He's hungry and he's mean."

The dinosaur lifts one leg to take a step. You're afraid of being trampled.

*If you climb onto the dinosaur's foot so you don't get stepped on, turn to* **page 30.**

*If you lie very still, turn to* **page 36.**

"It's time to wake up now," says Max.

You're still shaking with fear. But when you open your eyes, the dinosaur is gone. In fact, you're back in Max's workshop, lying on his sofa.

"How did you save me from the dinosaur?" you ask. "And how did you get the time beamer to work without the key?"

Max's eyes twinkle. "My little experiment worked," he chuckles. "You see, there is no time beamer. The machine is an ordinary tape recorder. I used the red key to hypnotize you. Then I simply guided you on a little dream trip."

*Turn to* **page 26.**

At first you're angry. But Max looks so pleased that you have to smile. "The dream seemed awfully real to me," you say. You start to stand up, but your leg really hurts. You are amazed to see that it is red and sore!

Is Max telling the truth?

You'll never know for sure.

## THE END

You climb up the cliff. You're near the top, but you want to avoid the flying creature. You move a hundred feet to the right until you come to a cave entrance. You can't go any farther, so you pull yourself over the top of the cliff.

You almost step on *another* nest. It is filled with eggs, the size of footballs. Wow! What a terrific find. Uncle Max will be so pleased if you bring him one.

You reach for an egg. Then you notice a really weird dinosaur in the distance. He has a horn on his nose, like a rhinocerous. And long spikes all around his head. He looks clumsy and slow.

*If you take the egg and run,*
*turn to* **page 34.**

*If you don't want to take any chances*
*and hide in the cave until the*
*dinosaur goes away, turn to* **page 38.**

**28**

"You don't have to shout," Max says, getting to his feet. "As soon as I finish these notes," he begins. . . .

You lose your temper. "WE'RE LEAVING RIGHT NOW!" you scream.

"All right, all right," says Max, getting out the time beamer and turning the key. "The power is a little weak," he says. "We can give it a try. But I can't promise we'll get back to the present. If you want to wait instead, I might be able to fix the battery."

*If you take your chances and try the time beamer, turn to* **page 39.**

*If you decide to wait, hoping Max can fix the machine, turn to* **page 32.**

Whew! That was a close call!

You're back in the workshop again. Alamo is exploring the cluttered room. And Max is already at his desk, writing in a notebook.

You pat Alamo good-bye and start the long walk home.

You reach the edge of town and realize that you are being followed. You wheel around and bump into Alamo.

"Alamo! What are you doing here?" you scold. But secretly you're pleased. Alamo licks your face, and nuzzles your neck. If only you could keep him!

*Turn to* **page 55.**

You sit on the dinosaur's foot. He starts walking.

WHOMP! WHOMP! WHOMP! Each time he takes a step, you almost fall off. You squeeze tighter, trying to hold on. But the dinosaur notices you now. He leans down with his mouth open. There are big spaces between his long, sharp teeth. He takes your leg in his mouth and raises his head again.

Higher and higher you go. Soon you're getting close to Max, who is still holding onto the dinosaur's weak arm. Max stretches out a hand to you.

*Go on to next page.*

If you don't act fast, you'll be eaten.
But is Max strong enough to hold your weight? If he isn't, you'll both be lost.

You also get another idea. You remember the spaces between the dinosaur's teeth. You could start kicking and hope your foot will slip through.

*If you grab Max's hand,*
*turn to* **page 40.**

*If you decide to kick to get your foot*
*free, turn to* **page 46.**

**32**     You decide to see if Max can fix the time beamer. Max empties his pockets and sits down. He stares at the piles of junk. There is a mound of carrot sticks, a jar of peanut butter, and all kinds of wire and screws.

"I've got it!" he says finally. "I'll make a solar cell to power the time beamer."

Half an hour later, the time beamer is fixed. Max inserts the key and twists.

BLLLLLLLISSSSST. BOOOOM. RAH.

*Turn to* **page 35.**

"I'm jumping," you yell to Max.

You step off the edge of the cloud. Max stretches out his arms and catches you. A moment later the mist lifts and you are both sitting on the floor of his workshop.

Max opens up the time beamer and fiddles with some wires. Then he pops in two new batteries. "The machine should work perfectly now."

Max sits down at his desk and starts writing very fast.

"Can I borrow the time beamer?" you ask.

Max mumbles something but he doesn't look up.

You put the time beamer in your pocket and start for home. Maybe you'll take it to school tomorrow for show and tell.

Back in your house, you decide to read the comic strips in the Sunday paper. As you turn the pages, a headline catches your eye:

*Turn to* **page 52.**

**34**    You pick up an egg. It's pretty heavy. You keep an eye on the dinosaur as you walk away. Suddenly it lowers its head and charges. Its short fat legs move fast. But you still have time to get away.

You throw down the egg and start to run.

SPLAT. You step in the yolk and slip . . . right over the edge of the cliff. You're covered with gooey egg now. You try to hold onto a branch, but it slips out of your fingers. Down . . . down . . . down you go.

Better luck next time!

**THE END**

This time the trip is noisy. And it isn't over in a flash. You and Max stand side by side on a hazy greenish cloud. You seem to be speeding straight down a dimly lit tunnel. It feels as if you're in an elevator that's dropping fast.

You feel a jolt and stumble to your knees. Max has disappeared! You peer over the edge of the cloud and see that he is now ten feet below you on another cloud. "Max, what's happening?" you shout.

"You've fallen behind in time," Max explains. "But I don't think it's too serious. If you want, though, you can jump down here and join me."

You want to make sure you get back to the present. But what will happen if you miss Max's cloud? Will you be stuck in this hazy green place forever?

*If you decide to jump down to Max, turn to* **page 33.**

*If you stay where you are, turn to* **page 50.**

You lie very still. The dinosaur takes a step. His foot comes down right next to your head. Then you notice his tail. With every step, it sweeps back and forth like a giant broom.

Desperately you start digging a hole in the sand. In a moment, the tail will smash you to smithereens.

WHACK!

You'd better move fast. If you don't, no one will ever know about your incredible dinosaur adventures.

**THE END**

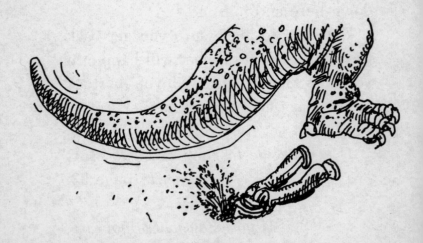

Ten minutes later you stop to rest. Max gets out his peanut butter and carrot sticks.

You are annoyed. "How can you eat at a time like this?" you ask.

Calmly, Max opens the jar of peanut butter and begins to eat. Not long after, you hear branches snapping in the woods behind him.

Alamo's head appears over Max's shoulder. He drops the red key, then sticks his nose into the peanut butter jar.

Max smiles. "These creatures have a keen sense of smell. I knew he'd come back for more."

You pick up the key. "Let's get out of here while we can."

"If you insist," says Max. "But Alamo should stay here where he belongs."

You try to shoo Alamo away. But he won't leave you. Finally you throw the peanut butter jar as far as you can, and Alamo runs off after it.

Max puts the key into the time beamer and twists it. . . .

Turn to page 42.

**38**     You decide to wait inside the cave. When your eyes get used to the light, you see dozens of eggs. They are twice as big as footballs.

"Pitipeet . . . pitipeep." You hear squeaky sounds coming from the eggs.

CRACK. An egg splits open. Then another . . . and another. Soon you're surrounded by a dozen baby dinosaurs. They are already up to your waist.

You try to leave the cave, but they surround you, begging for food. You try to fight your way out, but it's no use. They think you're their mother!

Soon you're exhausted. You sit down and watch the dinosaurs play. You're trapped!

Can this *really* be . . .

**THE END**

"Let's go back now," you say to Max.

"All right," he answers. "But I'm warning you. I just don't know what will happen."

Max puts the key into the time beamer and twists. Everything happens slowly this time. You feel like you are whirling through space. Then you see a blur of color. It looks like a movie going too fast.

"Oh, dear," says Max. "We're slowing down too soon. . . ."

The moving pictures finally stop.

*Turn to* **page 47.**

You grab Max's hand. Now you're stretched between Max and the dinosaur's mouth. The creature keeps raising its head. You think you're going to break in two. Then your sneaker slips off your trapped foot. You're free!

Max manages to hold you up until you balance yourself next to him.

"I wonder what comes next," says Max.

"Leave it to me," you say. "Hold tight while I climb onto your back."

You take Max's walking stick and climb onto his shoulders. The dinosaur can reach you now.

"Are you crazy?" Max yells. "He'll eat you!"

*Go on to the next page.*

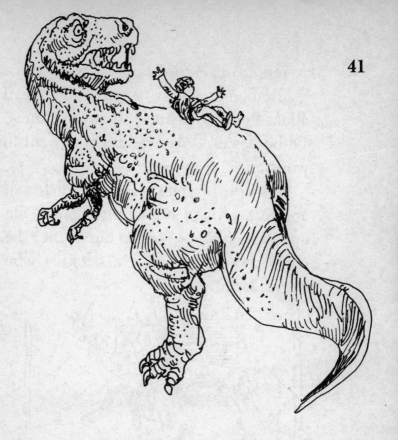

Sure enough, the dinosaur reaches for you. But you slip the walking stick between his jaws. The creature roars with rage, but he can't shut his mouth.

You both slide down the dinosaur's back, then run as fast as you can.

*Turn to* **page 37.**

You are back in Max's workshop.

"Remember," says Max, "not a word about the time beamer. If anyone knew, I'd be pestered day and night. I want to work on it in peace."

"It's a deal," you say and start to leave. You're tired and want to go home. You open the door and a man bursts into the room. It's Dr. Dooley, a scientist who works for Max.

*Go on to the next page.*

"We just received an amazing report. **43**
Our best scientist claims he has found
a jar of peanut butter with an Alamosaurus fossil. How do you explain a crazy
thing like that?"

"Beats me," says Max.

When Dr. Dooley leaves, Max looks
at you and smiles. Then you both laugh
and laugh.

## THE END

**44**  The taller man takes off his plastic helmet. "What's wrong with you two!" he scolds. "Everyone knows the air isn't fit for breathing! . . . Where's your oxygen . . . and which satellite are you from, anyway?"

Max clears his throat. He introduces himself and explains that you come from the past.

"I suppose you must be telling the truth," says the shorter man. "No one lives on Earth anymore."

"What happened?" Max asks.

"It's a long story," the tall man says, "but Earth died about two hundred years ago. We all live on gigantic satellites circling the planet. They're beautiful places, as you'll see. Every year or so we come back and take air samples. But so far there's been no improvement."

*Go on to the next page.*

Max turns to you. "Don't worry," he
says. "I'm sure we'll have a good time
while we're here. Besides, with a little
help from our new friend, I'll invent another time beamer."

The tall man nods.

"Just as soon as we get to Zakbar 999,
we'll set you up in a lab. And you'll each
get a personal robot to keep you com-
pany. When you return to your own time,
you can take the robots with you."

Wow! A robot! "Gee, thanks, mister,"
you say. You look out the window at the
stars. In the distance you see a meteor
shower, which sparkles like fireworks.

You're beginning to believe that Max
is right. This trip to the future will be
a great adventure. Just think, soon you'll
have your very own robot!

**THE END**

You kick as hard as you can. But the dinosaur's teeth clamp down harder. Then he tosses his head. You flip up and land in his mouth. It's all over now. Any second you'll be eaten alive.

"HEEEEELP!" you scream. In terror you watch the sharp, gleaming teeth get closer and closer. . . .

*Turn to* **page 25.**

You're standing in front of a corral filled with horses. Above the corral is a wooden sign:

## RIDERS WANTED FOR
## THE PONY EXPRESS

Max looks at the sign. "It must be 1860. Not bad. Not bad at all. We very nearly made it back to the present!"

You're glad you landed in the Wild West. It's a lot more fun than getting stuck in the Ice Age. And you already know how to ride a horse.

*Turn to* **page 48.**

*Turn to* **page 48.**

Max's eyes twinkle mischievously. "Just think of all the things I could invent! A simple toaster would make us rich and famous!" Suddenly he looks gloomy. "We'll need some money to begin with, though. That could be a real problem."

"I have an idea," you say. "I'll earn money by riding for the Pony Express!"

And that's just what you do.

You always enjoyed playing cowboy. Now you can see what it's really like!

### THE END

You decide to stay where you are. You watch Max drift farther and farther away from you. Soon he disappears in the greenish haze.

You're getting worried. Then you feel the cloud hit something solid. The haze lifts slowly.

You can't believe your eyes. You're standing on the stage at school. You're in the middle of a spelling bee.

*Go on the the next page.*

Two months ago, you were a finalist in the city-wide spelling bee. You lost in the last round.

Now you have another chance. Your turn is coming up. Your teacher says the word, and you break into a big grin. How could you have made a mistake last time?

You say each letter slowly and clearly: "D . . . I . . N . . O . . . S . . . A . . . U . . . R."

You're the winner! The prize is a beautiful brass trophy. But best of all, you get to live the next two months a second time.

**THE END**

# THE WINNING NUMBER FOR NOODLE DOODLES' SUPER SWEEPSTAKES IS 9878989.

Suddenly you get a great idea. You write the number down, and then walk to the candy store where they sell tickets for the contest.

You make sure that no one is watching. Then you set the time beamer for last month. With a twist of the key, you zip backward thirty days. Then you buy your ticket and write in the winning number. Again, you use the time beamer to return to the present.

*Go on to the next page.*

You walk back home.

Your mother runs to meet you in the front yard. She gives you a big hug. "Guess what happened?" she says. "You won the Super Sweepstakes!"

You pretend to be surprised. Then she tells you about the grand prize.

It isn't exactly what you expected. But it's still very nice. You've won a lifetime supply of Noodle Doodles. And a free trip to Disneyland every year for the rest of your life!

**THE END**

You're not ready for another adventure. Max uses the time beamer to take you back to the present.

Back in the lab, Max piles his bones in the middle of the room. "Do you have any samples with you?" he asks. "Everything should be tested in the laboratory."

"I didn't find any bones," you say. "But I did take these," and you show Max the glittery stones you found.

Max looks at them under his microscope. "These are of no scientific interest. They are only ordinary diamonds."

"DIAMONDS!!!" you shout. "But doesn't that mean we're rich?"

Max looks surprised. "Why didn't I think of that?" he asks, scratching his head. "We're rich, all right. *Very* rich."

### THE END

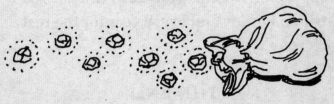

When you reach your house, you open the gate to your large backyard and let Alamo in. The yard is fenced in, so Alamo should be safe.

"Just in time for supper, honey," your mother calls as you enter the house. "Hurry up and wash."

You join your parents at the kitchen table and begin to eat.

"Your birthday is next week, you know," your mother says. "Do you still want that spotted pony we saw at your cousin's farm?"

*Turn to* **page 56.**

You choke on your food. Somehow it's hard to explain that you've changed your mind. Finally you blurt out the words, "I've been thinking . . . I know he looks a little funny . . . but he's really special. . . ."

"Finish chewing," your father interrupts. "If you mean you want some other kind of pet, that's fine, too."

Your heart soars. "Really?" you ask. And your parents smile and nod.

Alamo must have heard your voice. Just then he sticks his head through the open window.

"Mom, Pop . . . meet Alamo," you say proudly. "He's a little different, but I know we'll all be friends!"

**THE END**

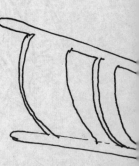

**58**    The flying creature takes you to the top of a cliff. As you get closer, you see a nest filled with eggs. A tall animal stands over the nest. He looks like a giant ostrich without any feathers. He smashes open a large egg with his claw. Then he eats it.

The flying creature screams with rage, then swoops down to protect its nest. As the creature attacks, it drops you.

*Turn to* **page 5.**